DR. ELEVENTH

originated by Roger Hargreaves

Written and illustrated by Adam Hargreaves

It had been a very busy day.

A very busy day filled with danger.

Even the Doctor, whose life was filled with danger, could hardly remember a more unpleasant day.

He sipped his tea, and then an awful thought occurred to him.

"Bother! I have left something behind," he said to River Song.

"We are going to have to go back and retrace our footsteps until we find it!"

"Don't be daft!" exclaimed River. "I'm not going through all that danger all over again. Once was bad enough!"

"But what I left behind is vital!"

"Why don't we just go back in time and get whatever you have lost?" asked River. "After all, we do have a time machine."

"The trouble is, I can't remember where in time I lost it," explained the Doctor.

"All right then, sweetie. Off we go."

"Quick, follow me," said River, climbing a wall.

"But that's not the way we went last time," said the Doctor.

"Maybe not, but we need to avoid the Zygons."

"What Zygons?" asked the Doctor.

"Those Zygons!" called River, as the two rabbits suddenly transformed into Zygons.

"Yowza!" shrieked the Doctor, scrambling up the wall behind River.

"Gosh," said the Doctor, following River across a rope bridge. "You never know when a Zygon is going to pop up next."

"That's the trouble with Zygons," said River. "One minute you're looking at a cute rabbit and the next it's a deadly Zygon."

"This way, sweetie," said River.

"Geronimo!" cried the Doctor as he tried to catch up.

"And look out for those Silurians!" called River.

The Doctor pulled himself up and barely swung over their heads.

River laughed. "I don't know how you'd ever get along without me."

"I'm perfectly capable of coping on my own," huffed the Doctor . . . who promptly fell through a hole in the roof.

"Heeeelp!" he cried.

"You were saying . . . ," said River, jumping through after him.

The Doctor and River landed on the floor of an ancient temple.

"Any sign of what you're looking for?" asked River.

"No, but I do remember we came this way before. Look . . ."

"It's the Weeping Angels! Remember, look, but don't blink. Blink . . . ," began the Doctor.

". . . and we are dead. Yes, I know, I know," finished River.

She and the Doctor cautiously made their way past the Angel statues, making sure that they did not take their eyes off them.

To look away would have caused terrible trouble.

One might say that in the blink of an eye they escaped the Weeping Angels, but one blink of an eye would have been enough to allow the statues to come alive and attack them.

So there was no blinking of any eyes.

However, once they had safely escaped the Angels, they were faced with a new danger.

Snakes!

A whole pit full of snakes.

"I was really hoping you might have found what you were looking for before we got here," said River.

"I hate snakes!" she added.

"There, it's not so bad, is it?" asked the Doctor.

River gave the Doctor a withering look.

"Whatever it is you have left behind had better be worth it!"

The snakes hissed in agreement.

And River shuddered.

"Onwards and upwards," said the Doctor, climbing a vine out of the pit.

"I remember this cave," said the Doctor. "This is where we saw the giant spider. Now . . . what did we do next?"

"We ran!" shrieked River, spotting the giant spider lurking in a corner of the cave.

And she and the Doctor ran.

And ran.

And ran some more.

As fast as their legs would carry them.

Which, as you might imagine when you are being chased by a giant spider, is very fast indeed!

They escaped the spider, and River was trying to remember what horror came next when the Doctor suddenly stopped.

"Here it is!" he cried jubilantly.

And there on the ground was a hat.

A fez hat.

The Doctor's fez hat.

"I don't believe it!" exclaimed River. "You made me go through all of that all over again for a hat!"

"But it's my favorite hat," said the Doctor sheepishly.

The Doctor and River finally got back to the TARDIS.

And for the second time that day, they settled down to a nice cup of tea.

In fact, there was nothing that they had not done for the second time that day.

"Gosh!" exclaimed the Doctor. "Where did I put my hat?"

River looked up in consternation and then she laughed.

"It's on your head, silly!"